The Miss Meow Pageant

Story by

Richardo Keens-Douglas

Art by

Marie Lafrance

Annick Press
Toronto • New York

Designed by Marielle Maheu

Annick Press Ltd.

We acknowledge the support of the Canada Council for the Arts for our publishing program. We also thank the Ontario Arts Council.

Cataloguing in Publication Data
Keens-Douglas, Richardo
The Miss Meow pageant

ISBN 1-55037-537-7 (bound) ISBN 1-55037-536-9 (pbk.)

I. Lafrance, Marie. II. Title.

PS8571.E44545M57 1998 jC813í.54 C98-930310-1
PZ7.K43Mi 1998

The art in this book was rendered in acrylics.
The text was typeset in Tekton and Litterbox ICG, with Mo Funky Fresh Symbols.

Distributed in Canada by:
Firefly Books Ltd.
3680 Victoria Park Avenue
Willowdale, ON
M2H 3K1

Published in the
U.S.A. by Annick Press (U.S.) Ltd.
Distributed in the U.S.A. by:
Firefly Books (U.S.) Inc.
P.O. Box 1338
Ellicott Station
Buffalo, NY 14205

Printed and bound in Canada by
Friesens, Altona, Manitoba.

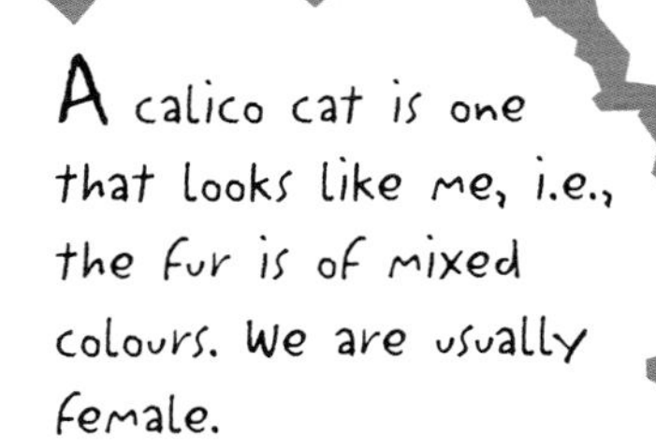

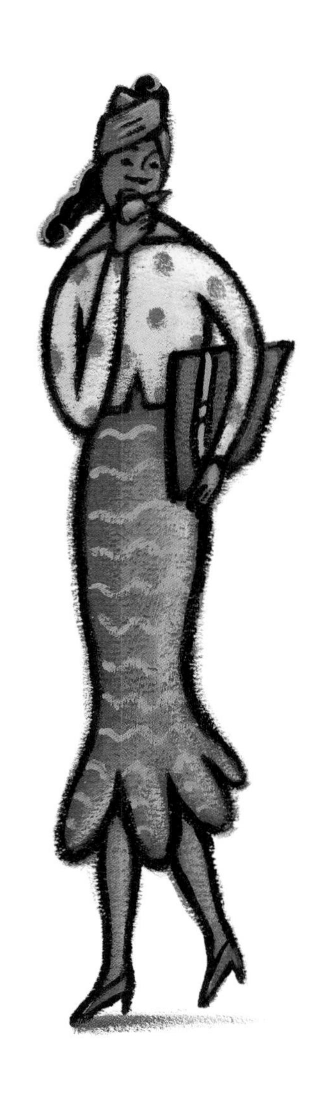

This story is dedicated
to all the teachers
who keep the heart laughing and
the imagination soaring.

Once upon a time there was a teacher called Henrietta Jones.

One day, on her way home from school, she suddenly got this eerie feeling that something or somebody was following her. So she quickly spun around. But there was no one, except for Margaret the butcher's wife way in the distance, and some children playing hopscotch on the side of the road.

She kept on walking, but this same feeling started to creep up her spine again.

She stopped, and this time she slowly turned around. And lo and behold, sitting in the middle of the road looking at her was one of the ugliest-looking cats you would ever come across in the feline world.

Before the cat could say "MEOW", some of the children started throwing things at it, and in the blinking of an eye the cat was gone.

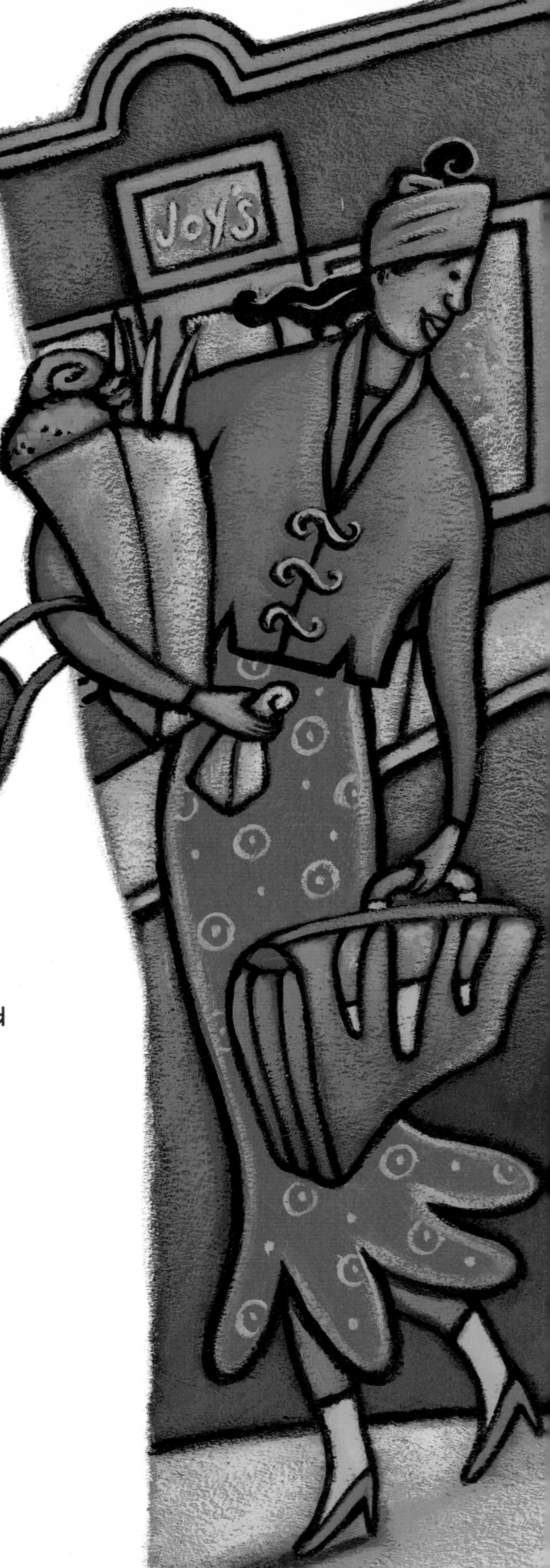

CHOICE MEAT
SAM'S

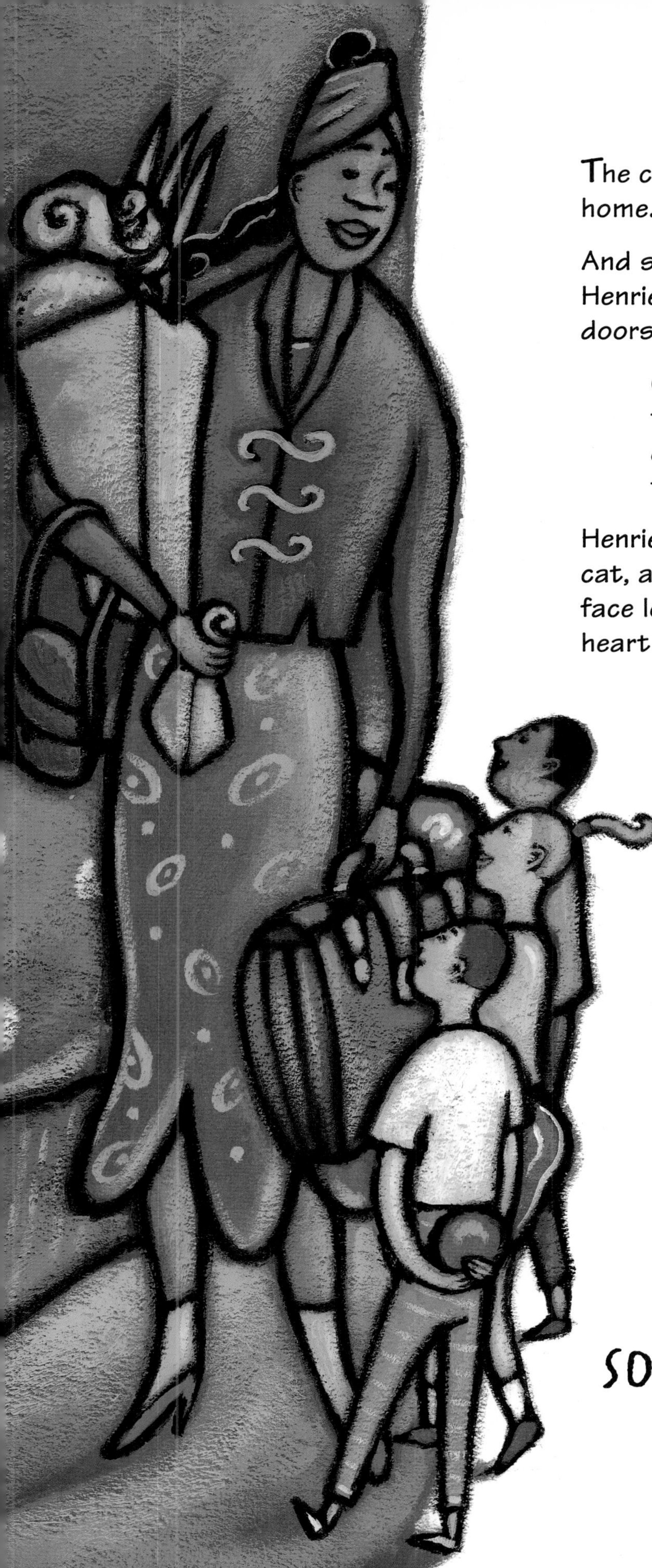

The children followed Henrietta home.

And sure enough, in front of Henrietta's house, sitting on her doorstep, was this same cat.

One of the children turned to her and asked, "Miss, does that ugly cat belong to you?"

Henrietta took a look at the cat, and a sad, frightened little face looked back at her, and her heart just melted.

"YES, THAT CAT BELONGS TO ME," she said.

And immediately it just relaxed and sprawled out in front of Henrietta's door like it had been living there for years.

Henrietta noticed that this cat had an uncertain colour.

It was somewhere between gold and brown, with a purplish tint, grey dots, black and white stripes, and two white squares around the eyes.

It looked like a cross between a punk and a confused zebra.

SO SHE NAMED THE CAT SPARROW.

One day, Henrietta's friend Len phoned her up to say he'd read in the newspapers that they were having a pussy-cat contest: "THE MISS MEOW PAGEANT".

"The Miss Who?" Henrietta asked.

"The Miss Meow Pageant. And you should enter Sparrow in the competition."

"Go on," said Henrietta. "I can't do that."

"Why not?"

"Because Sparrow is a tom cat, and you can't enter a tom cat in a Miss Meow Pageant."

"Never mind that," said Len. "A CAT IS A CAT IS A CAT. Nobody will know the difference."

"Anyway," Henrietta continued, "Sparrow is a liberated cat and he doesn't believe in all this beauty contest nonsense. Everyone is pretty in their own way."

"I understand where Sparrow is coming from," said Len. "But listen to where I'm coming from for a moment. If Sparrow wins, he'll be getting:

★ FIVE YEARS OF FREE KITTY LITTER.

★ FIVE YEARS OF THE BEST CAT FOOD. FREE.

★ HIS OWN PUSSY-CAT BASKET WITH HIS NAME ON IT.

And last but not least,

★ A FREE TRIP TO EUROPE FOR THE CAT AND ITS OWNERS FOR ONE WEEK.

Best of all,

THEY WILL CROWN HIM WITH A TIARA!"

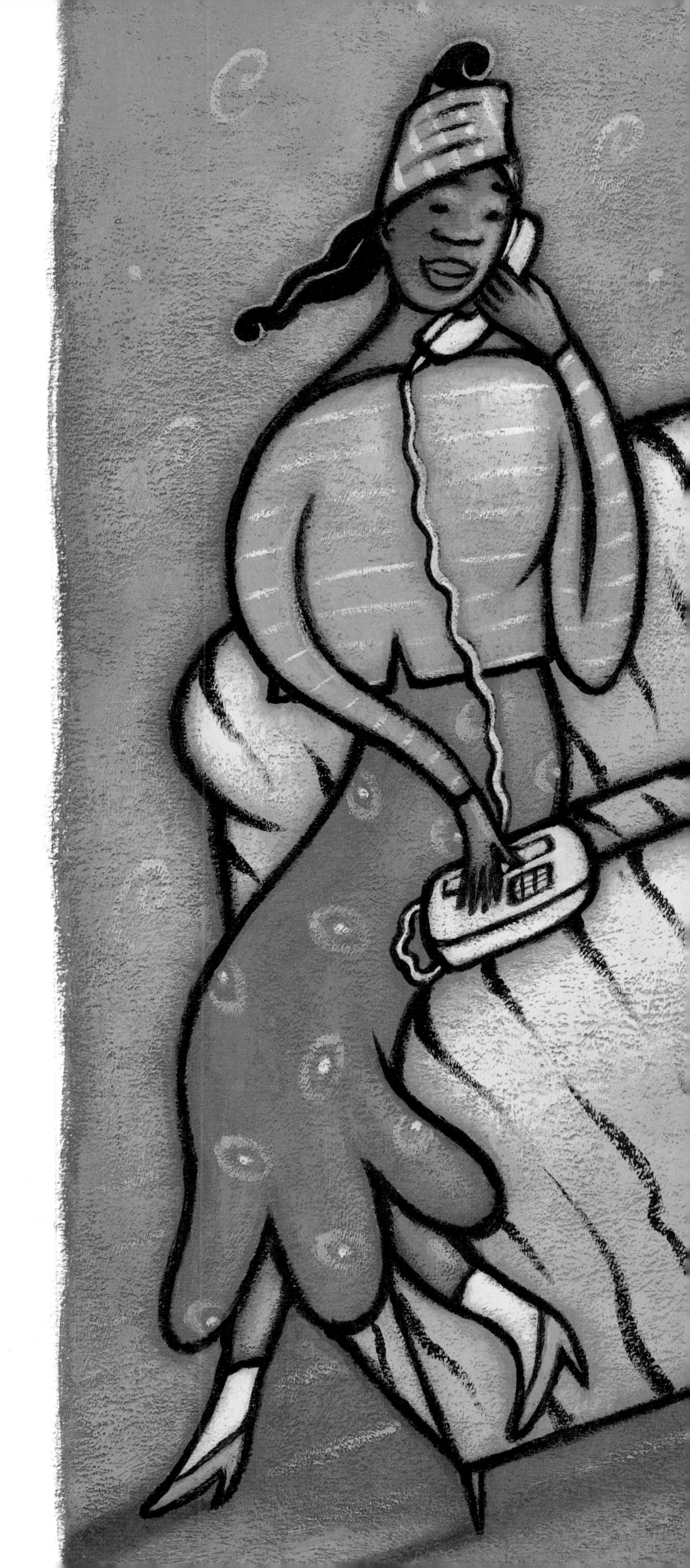

Well, when Henrietta heard of all the prizes, she said she would give it a thought.

That night Henrietta had a dream that Sparrow entered the competition and came last.

The following night she had another dream: that they discovered he was a tom cat and he got disqualified.

She told Len about her dreams.

"NOT TO WORRY," said Len. "That's a good sign. Because when you have a dream like that, the opposite always happens. So that means he's going to win."

A week later Len came to visit Henrietta, all excited. "This is going to be the biggest feline contest in the whole country," he said. "All kinds of fancy cats will be entering, so we have to prepare Sparrow. We must teach him how to walk properly on the stage."

Sparrow just looked at him and rolled his eyes.

Henrietta said, "WALK? How do you mean, WALK?"

"If Sparrow had a walk like yours or mine he would win hands down," Len said. "We'll have to coach him."

First of all they put on a Lawrence Welk tape. Sparrow immediately closed his eyes and fell asleep.

Next they tried Tina Turner, followed by Michael Jackson, classical, jazz. Nothing moved Sparrow. Not even a twitch of his tail.

Then Henrietta put on some music by her favourite singer: The Mighty Sparrow, Calypso King of the World.

And right away Sparrow stood up and stretched his body.

He watched them carry on for about two songs. Then a song called "Jean and Dinah, Rosita and Clementina" came on.

Sparrow jumped off the sofa and he started to follow Len.

Len was overjoyed. He shouted, "That's the song we will use." And he started to sing along.

"JEAN AND DINAH, ROSITA AND CLEMENTINA."

Well, the big night of the pageant arrived.

THE EXCITEMENT!
THE PEOPLE!

The stage was beautifully decorated, bathed in bright, colourful light.

Henrietta was backstage with Sparrow, getting ready.

Len had a front-row seat, dead centre, since he didn't want to miss a thing.

He was sitting next to a Rasta who also had a cat in the competition – called "ITAL".

Then, without warning, the lights started to fade and the room got quiet.

The music started. The stage lights came on, and on walked the first cat. Jet black.

Then a Siamese cat, then a cat in a sombrero.

Next, a white, fluffy cat with five pink bows on its tail waltzed on.

Then the music switched to reggae and the cat with the dreadlocks came.

The Rasta shouted, "DAT'S MY CAT MAN. ITAL!"

There were different breeds and colours.

They had a bow-legged cat with sunglasses on.

There was one that refused to walk. The owner had to carry it all the way.

There was even one that looked like a real tiger and escaped into the audience. People laughed.

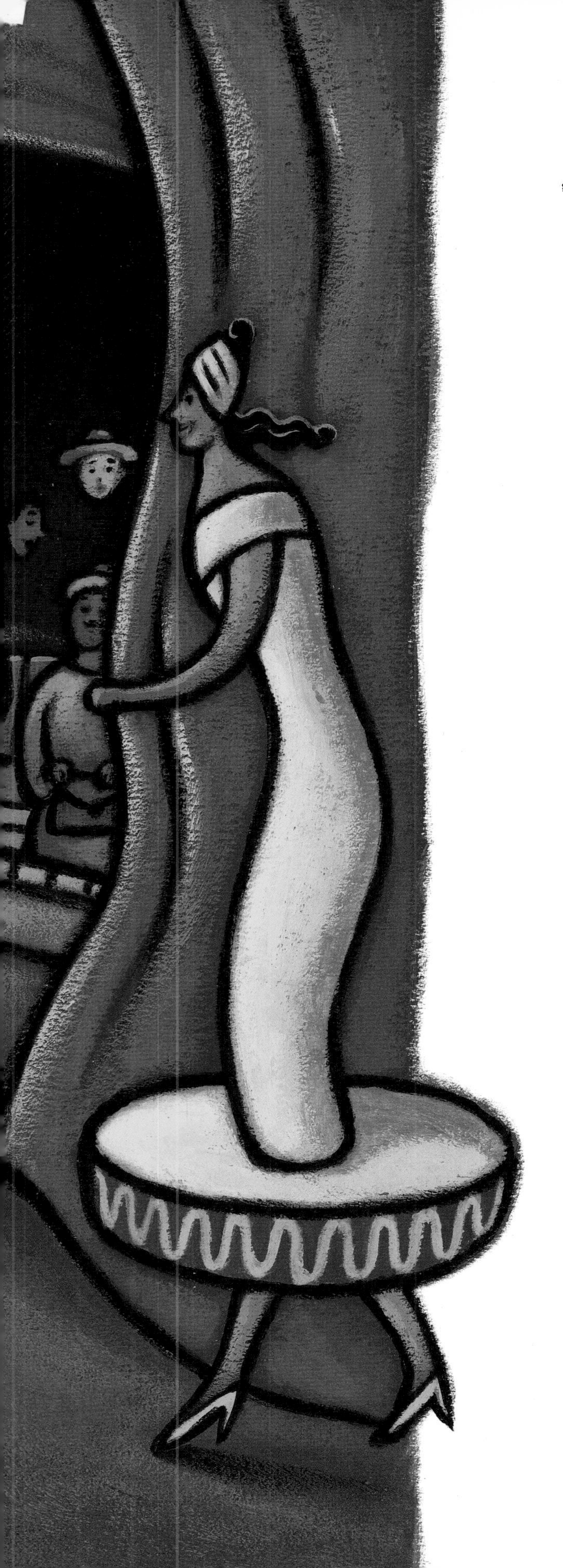

Then the music for Jean and Dinah started.

Len got very quiet.

Henrietta appeared on stage, but Sparrow was nowhere to be seen.

Almost all the lights went off, and just one spot remained on the stage.

Len said, "Lord. Power failure."

But Henrietta had planned that.

Then Sparrow just walked out from behind Henrietta and stepped right into the spotlight and sat down on his two hind legs.

A woman sitting next to Len said, "IF THAT IS A CAT, THAT'S THE UGLIEST-LOOKING CAT I EVER SEEN IN MY LIFE."

Everyone started to laugh at poor Sparrow.

Len cringed in his seat.

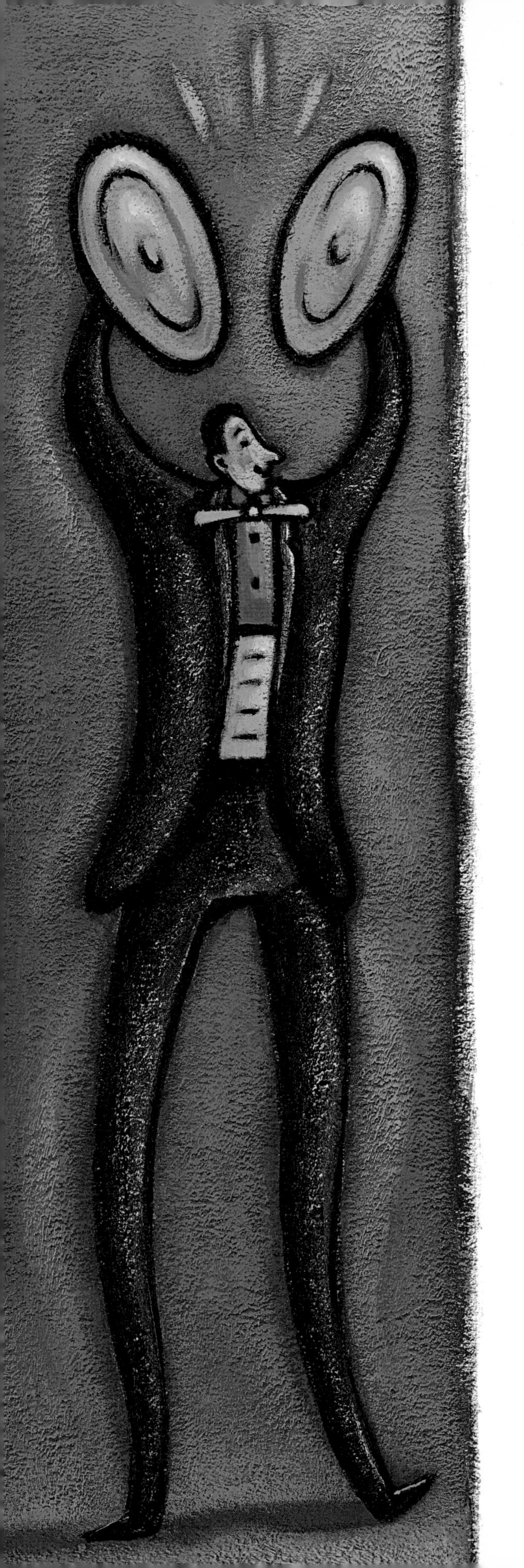

Then, with the clash of a cymbal, the stage filled with beautiful light again.

And Sparrow stood up, looked at the audience with pride and started to walk down the ramp.

He was walking a little bit like Len and a little bit like Henrietta.

When the pretty lights hit Sparrow's coat, it was like magic.

The gold and the brown began to shine.

The black and white stripes were moving with his body like they had a life of their own.

The two white squares around his eyes started to glow.

The audience began mumbling.

Then Sparrow stopped, lay down, gave two, three little jerks with his body, got back up and started to walk again.

THE AUDIENCE SHOUTED, "WOOAAAAAAAAHHHH!"

He paused again. Looked to the left and to the right.

Then he turned around to see where Henrietta was.

And when he turned, the grey dots looked like silver. The purplish tint shimmered.

Everyone applauded.

SPARROW LOOKED MAGNIFICENT!

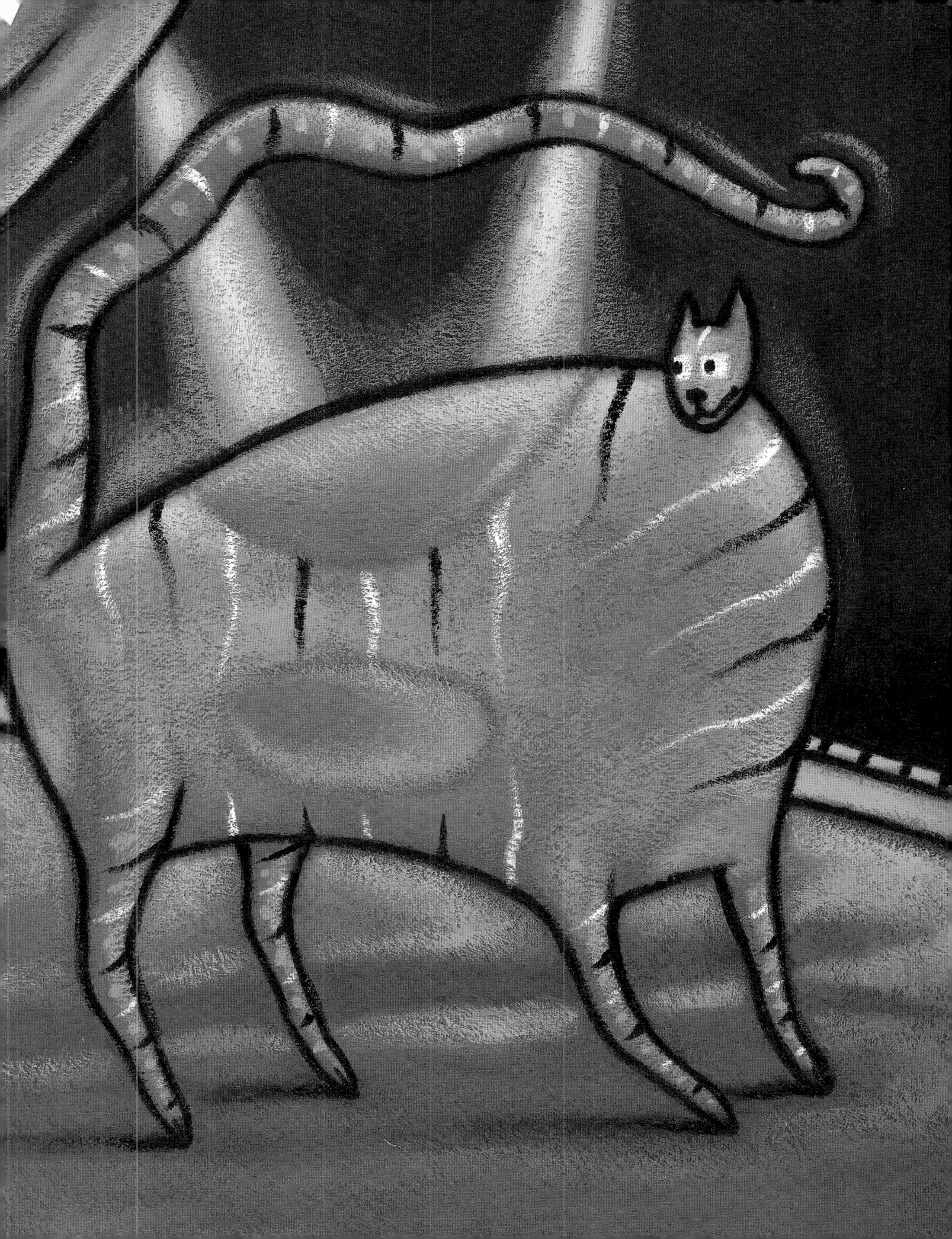

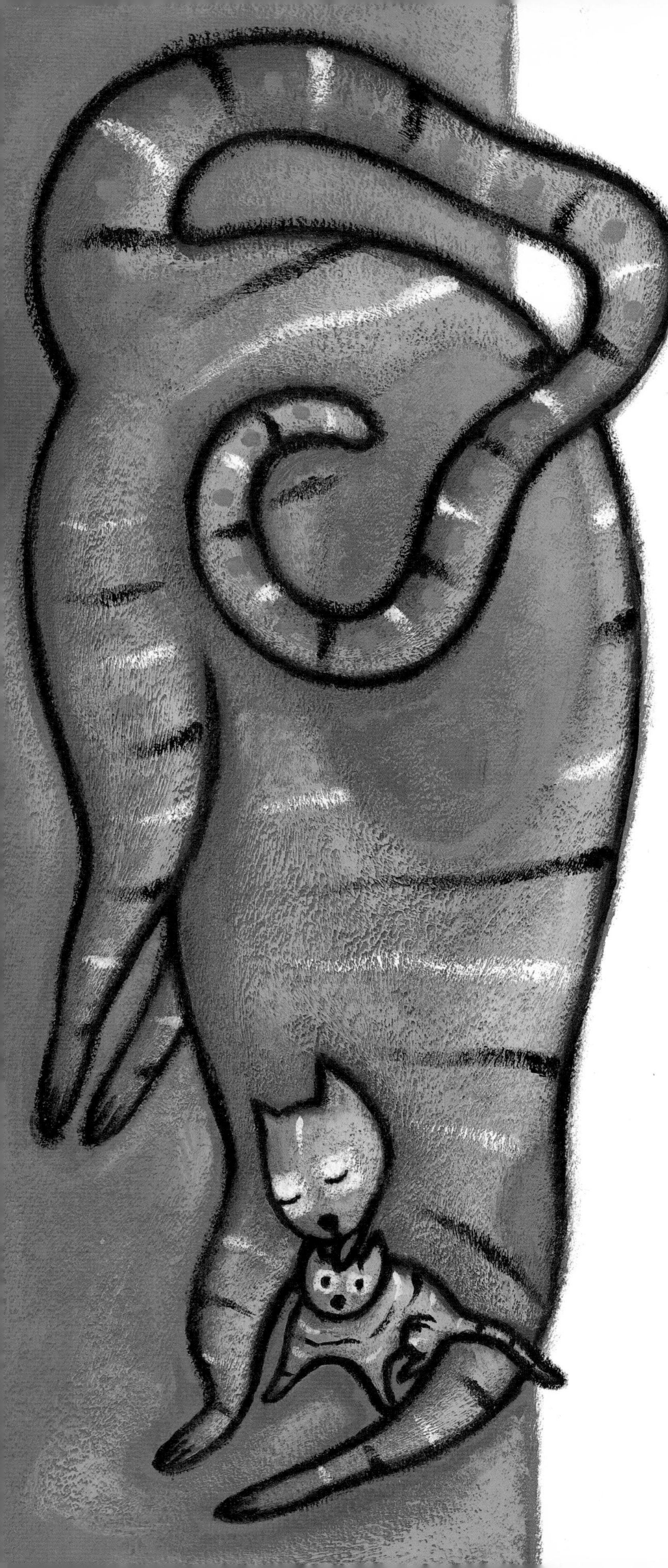

He continued walking to the front of the ramp.

When he reached the footlights, he lay down and gave one of the loudest purrs ever heard, and all of a sudden a little kitten appeared on stage.

Sparrow was not a boy at all.

SHE WAS A MOTHER.

The audience went wild.

Standing ovation.

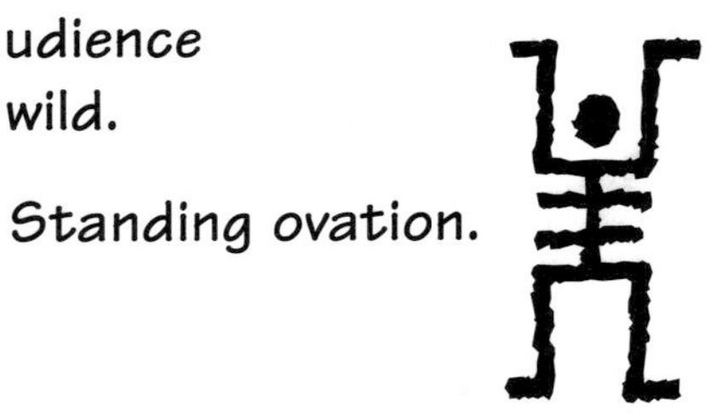

The kitten was just beautiful.

A little black and white, well, yes, and grey dots.

And gold and brown with a purplish tint.

A CALICO KITTEN.

SPARROW WAS CROWNED THE WINNER.

Sparrow made everybody happy that night.

WHAT A NIGHT THAT WAS!

(And right now, Len, Henrietta, Sparrow and the kitten are in Europe, prowling around.)